BABY DRAG QUEEN

C.A. TANAKA

orca soundings

ORCA BOOK PUBLISHERS

Published in Canada and the United States
in 2023 by Orca Book Publishers.
orcabook.com

Library and Archives Canada Cataloguing in Publication
Title: Baby drag queen / C.A. Tanaka.
Names: Tanaka, Candie, author.
Series: Orca soundings.
Description: Series statement: Orca soundings
Identifiers: Canadiana (print) 20220239843 | Canadiana (ebook) 20220239851 |
ISBN 9781459835320 (softcover) | ISBN 9781459835337 (PDF) |
ISBN 9781459835344 (EPUB)
Classification: LCC PS8639.A5598 B33 2023 | DDC jC813/.6—dc23

Library of Congress Control Number: 2022938247

Summary: In this high-interest accessible novel for teen readers,
seventeen-year-old Ichiro secretly enters a drag-performance contest.

Orca Book Publishers is committed to reducing the consumption
of nonrenewable resources in the production of our books. We make
every effort to use materials that support a sustainable future.

Orca Book Publishers gratefully acknowledges the support
for its publishing programs provided by the following agencies:
the Government of Canada, the Canada Council for the Arts and
the Province of British Columbia through the BC Arts Council
and the Book Publishing Tax Credit.

Edited by Tanya Trafford
Design by Ella Collier
Cover photography by Pexels/Kamaji Ogino

Printed and bound in Canada.

26 25 24 23 • 1 2 3 4

For all the baby drag performers

out there—stay bright!

Chapter One

It's 4:00 a.m. Ichiro hears the phone ring, his mother's hushed voice. He rolls over and goes back to sleep. Around ten he pulls on a pair of shorts, throws on a white T-shirt and heads downstairs. It's Saturday, so he's hoping his mom will make him breakfast. But she's not in the kitchen.

"Mom!" he yells. "Mom?"

"Ichiro, I'm here." She's taking a load of laundry out of the washer and dryer they share with their landlord. "Not so loud—the neighbors might hear you."

"I'm hungry," he says.

"Okay, okay," she replies.

At almost seventeen, he should be making his own breakfast. But breakfast is one of the only times they get to sit down and talk. He wishes she could be around more.

"Ichiro, why so late this morning?" She's dressed for her shift at the restaurant.

"Ten isn't late, Mom. Some kids sleep till noon," he says. He rests his head on the kitchen table.

"No, no, they don't."

"Yes, they do."

"What would you like today?" she asks.

"Pancakes and bacon," he says hopefully.

"Yeesh, so much work. How about a cheese omelet with bacon?"

"Mom!"

"Ichiro, no complaining. You should be cooking for your mother."

She puts the frying pan on the stove and breaks two eggs into a bowl. She preheats the oven and puts four slices of bacon on parchment paper.

"Who called last night?" he asks.

"Grandma."

"Grandma Ito? What did she say? Can I go visit? I still haven't been to Japan."

"No, Grandpa is sick. He fell and is in the hospital." His mother opens the oven and turns away from Ichiro. When she does this, he knows she's crying.

"He's not doing well, and she wants me to go home. But how can I?"

"Mom, I'm going to be working soon. Maybe I can help?"

She doesn't answer. She puts the omelet on a plate and puts it in front of him. "How's school?" she asks.

"Okay."

"Why just okay? What's wrong?"

"Changing schools is hard, Mom. I miss Jazz and Blaze. I don't fit in with the Japanese kids because I can't speak Japanese. But I can't speak Mandarin either. Why did you and dad not teach me anything?"

"Ichiro, I can't speak Japanese. The girls at school used to pick on me too. They pulled my pigtails and pushed me off my bike. It's just how it is."

"Pulled your pigtails?" Ichiro laughs.

"It's not funny," she says. But she's smiling.

"It's hard to imagine you in pigtails."

"Why don't you join an after-school club and make some new friends?"

"Only nerds do that."

"You have Chris and Jia."

Ichiro pushes the eggs away from the bacon. He likes to keep his foods separate.

"What about all those books you read?" his mother says.

Ichiro loves to read nonfiction to learn new things. He doesn't like what he calls "the pretend world of fiction."

"What about them?"

"Hang out in the library. Find a girl who reads."

"No thanks. What I want is a new skateboard."

"Honey, I can't afford that."

"Mom, I can pay for it myself."

"With what?"

"I signed up for cafeteria class this year. The teacher is supposed to be a great chef. We learn how to make giant pots of soup, salads and desserts for the students. And they offer some part-time work helping with catering the banquets at night after school."

She clears his plate. "Maybe then you can help out a bit more around here."

"Like how?" Ichiro asks.

"You know, cook for us sometimes?"

"We'll see, Mom. I am still a beginner."

"Confidence, daughter. You can do it," she says.

Ichiro feels weird when his mother calls him daughter. He has told her before that he doesn't feel like a daughter. But she didn't understand what he was saying, and he could tell she wasn't ready to have a serious talk. He knows it will have to happen sooner or later.

Ichiro's mom finally leaves for work, which means he can play some video games. He plays FIFA for a couple of hours and then takes a nap. When he wakes up, it surprises him to see that it's 5:00 p.m. already. Bored, he gets up and snoops in his mother's room.

Ichiro knows he shouldn't be in there, but his mother's room has always been a mystery to him, especially the very large and full closet. He never knows what he'll find in there. Last month he checked out some old dresses in the back that he can't remember ever seeing. She probably wore them way back when she met Dad. Ichiro moves the bulky winter coats and old hat boxes out of the way. He has to be super careful to put everything back in just the right way.

There's something on the other side of the closet that draws his attention. It's a big pile of clothes on the floor. Men's clothing and a couple of pairs of shoes. Must be clothing his dad left behind that Mom is finally going to get rid of. One day, when Ichiro was only six years old, his dad just got up and left. Though his mother tried to comfort him, Ichiro cried for a very long time. He used to think it was all his mother's fault. Now that he's older, he's realized his dad was never meant to have kids. He's too self-involved. Travel and photography have always been his passions. He's rarely even in the country anymore at all. Ichiro can't decide whether he loves or hates his dad. Sometimes it's a bit of both.

He sees his dad only a few times a year, when he's passing through town. His dad left Canada right after the breakup to do a photo shoot in Hong Kong. He's now a well-known artist in China. He got married again, to a woman who is kind but not the type who wants kids. Ichiro's friends think his dad is so cool. Ichiro just wishes he would visit more.

His dad says that the next time he visits, he'll take Ichiro to the futuristic exhibit of sneaker art at the Hexagon Gallery in North Vancouver. There are a bunch of Air Jordans on display that artists have taken to the next level. Most of the shoes are so cool-looking, but only for display. Ichiro and his dad will go for dim sum afterward at Ichiro's favorite restaurant, Jade Garden, in Chinatown.

Ichiro pulls out a vintage dress. It's purple and made of lightweight wool, with a pleated front and sleeves. The label is one he doesn't recognize. He pulls it over his T-shirt and shorts. He looks in the mirror and laughs. When he raises his arms, he looks like a large prehistoric bird ready for flight. But his side profile, with his arms down, looks rather elegant. He searches around for a pair of heels and accessories to complete the look. He wanders over to the vanity. So many tubes of lipstick! He pouts in front of the mirror. A nice purply red should fit his style. He purses his plump lips and smears a couple of light strokes across his mouth. He gets lost looking at himself in the mirror. "I can totally pull this off," he says to himself.

"Ichiro, Ichiro?" His mother is home early.

He rushes out of her room and into the bathroom down the hall. Did he remember to put everything back? Shit, he's still wearing the dress and heels. He quickly slips them off and hides them in the cupboard under the sink.

"I'm in the bathroom. Be right out." He quickly wipes the lipstick off his face and scrubs his lips with soap and water. It's so dark though. His heart is beating fast, and he feels hot. He can barely think. The room feels like it's spinning.

"Ichiro, are you okay?"

"Yes, fine. Be right there." He finds some makeup remover and dabs it on his lips, but they are still very red. He hears a sound.

It sounds like his mom is crying.

"Mom? Mom, are you okay?" he asks as he enters the kitchen. "What happened?" He puts his arms around her.

She wipes her eyes with the back of her hand. She won't look at him. "It's nothing, Ichiro."

"It's not nothing," he says. "Tell me!"

"I'm fine, I'm fine. Going to sleep now. Just tired."

"Mom!"

"See you in the morning." His mom looks at him, and he can see her swollen dark eyes. "What's that on your lips?" Of course she would notice, even in her state of distress. She sees everything.

Ichiro wipes his lips with the back of his hand. "Oh, that must be from the popsicle I had before you came home."

Chapter Two

In cafeteria class, Ichiro starts at the salad station. He washes the iceberg lettuce in the large stainless-steel sink by soaking it in a cold-water bath. He then swishes it around a bit before laying it out to dry on clean, dry towels. At the end of the cafeteria course, there's an opportunity to buy an official cookbook. It's a massive green hardcover book with "secret" cafeteria recipes for large crowds. Only students who go through the cooking course are able to buy it. Mr. Padanowski's classes are always full. He teaches students proper cooking and knife skills. He also goes over hygiene and safety in the kitchen. Today Ichiro is learning how to use an industrial dishwasher. He gently places the glassware and cutlery in the appropriate racks to make them shine.

If Ichiro works hard enough, he can help out with banquets in the evening. Sometimes he has to serve, and tonight it's his turn. They are cooking a bunch of game for a group of hunters. He feels nauseous washing the bear meat. There is so much blood, and thicker pieces still have black hair attached. He decides he will become a pescatarian, because he won't be able to enjoy meat after this.

Ichiro needs to earn more money to help his mom out. He has a little notebook where he keeps a tally of all his earnings, but he doesn't make very much. Mr. Padanowski told him that lots of restaurants downtown are looking for kitchen help.

He's promised to be a great reference for Ichiro because he knows how hard he works.

Ichiro rushes home after the banquet and goes straight to his room. He opens his laptop and starts looking for job openings. One of his favorite restaurants, Café Ivy, is looking for a dishwasher/kitchen help. It sounds perfect. Flexible shifts and free meals too! The ad mentions inclusivity in the workplace too, which is a bonus. There are few kitchen jobs that list that at all.

He can barely keep from screaming out loud. He fills out the online application as quickly as he can, really hoping they pick him.

———·———

The next morning is his birthday. Turning seventeen is a big deal to his mother, just like any birthday of his, but Ichiro figures it's just another day. Another day that his mother will try to make him feel better about his father not being around. She likes to make a fuss and usually buys a big cake for the two of them to share.

"Mom, I don't need a cake this year," says Ichiro as he comes into the kitchen. He hopes she won't take it the wrong way. He appreciates everything she does for him but knows they can use the money for other things.

"Don't be silly. Of course you do," she says. She shakes her head.

"It's not that important, Mom," he says.

When he gets home after school, he sees a card on the kitchen table with a note telling him to look in the fridge. There it is, a big white sponge cake topped with fresh fruit. His mom probably got it from the Chinese bakery down the road. It's his least favorite kind of cake. He would have much preferred a basic chocolate cake. He sighs and then sends his mom a text.

Thanks Mom. ❤

You're welcome! Home late tonight.

Ichiro sighs. His phone pings again. It's Chris.

Hey, where you at?

Hi.

What are you up to tonight?

Nothing.

It's your birthday, buddy! Let's go out!

———.———

Ichiro arrives early as usual. The Veggie Bistro is a tiny diner on Davie Street. Chris texts to say he's on his way. Ichiro scores a table near the window. He fishes out a coin from his pocket and selects a song on the mini jukebox.

A server approaches the table. "Hi, honey. You waiting for a friend? Can I get you a drink?"

"Yeah, just water for now, please."

The server slaps a couple of menus on the table. Where is Chris? Ichiro checks his phone again and then looks around. The bistro is a pillar of the queer community on Davie Street, though it has changed owners many times. The latest renos have been done in cotton-candy colors and give the place a happy, cheerful look. A complete gay overhaul.

Ichiro's phone rings.

"Hello?"

"Ichiro? It's Sarah from Café Ivy."

"Oh, hi!"

"We received your application and are short-staffed today. Any chance you can come in tonight and help out in the kitchen for a few hours? It'd be like a trial interview. If it works out, we'll keep you around."

"Uh...yeah, for sure! I'll be right there. Thirty minutes at the most."

"Great. Soon as you can."

Ichiro hangs up just as Chris walks through the door.

"Yo, buddy, happy birthday!" Chris gives him a homie handshake and pats his back.

"Thanks. Aw man, I'm sorry, but Café Ivy just called. I gotta go. They want me to work tonight."

"What? That's great. Go then. No worries. I'll grab some grub with Lexie."

Ichiro has no idea who that is, but as he gets up to leave, a girl approaches their table.

"Hey," Chris says.

"Hi," the girl says, looking at Ichiro.

"Hey," Ichiro mumbles. He stares, waiting to be introduced

"Oh, Ichiro, this is Lexie. She's new at school. Ichiro is just leaving. He's on his way to work." Chris winks at him.

"Uh, yeah, nice to meet you," Ichiro says. "Text you later, Chris."

He wants to stay but is also super excited about getting to the café. As he rushes out the door to catch the bus, Lexie comes running after him. "You forgot this," she says and slaps his hat onto his head.

"Thanks," he says a bit too eagerly.

"No problem." She pats his back. "See ya!" she says with a big smile.

Ichiro stands there for a minute. The bus goes rushing by, and he has to race to the stop. He's out of breath but makes it.

At Café Ivy he checks in with the host, and she takes him to the kitchen. "Hey," says a cook. "You must be Ichiro." He throws Ichiro an apron. "Wash up and then find me." The guy goes back to rushing from the oven to the pickup counter with food.

"You ever use one of these before?" he asks when Ichiro returns. He's talking about the dish-washing station.

"Yeah, no problem. We have this at our school cafeteria."

"Awesome. Here are the bins. Sort them out and start washing. Do a bunch of bowls first—everyone wants the clam chowder tonight for some reason."

Ichiro looks around for bowls in the bus bins and loads them in a rack. Then he takes the sprayer and gives them a quick rinse to remove food particles. Finally he feeds the rack into the main compartment. The grossest part is always the pre-soak of the flatware. He loads the cutlery into a flat rack, rinses it and pushes it through. It's not long before he's a sweaty mess. His T-shirt is soaked. He wipes the moisture from his forehead and brows.

"Hey, don't forget to wash up when it gets too hot," one of the cooks says. Ichiro walks over to the sink and mops his forehead with paper towels. Then he washes his hands well as they were taught in cafeteria class.

"What's your name?" asks the cook.

"Ichiro."

"Cool. That Japanese?"

It's so steamy Ichiro feels as if his face is going to melt. He turns to answer and knocks a glass onto the floor. Shards fly everywhere. "Oh shit," he says.

"No worries. But clean it up quick," the cook says. "I'm Sam. Kitchen is hot tonight. Drinks in the fridge on the far right, sodas and juice, if you're thirsty."

"Thanks," says Ichiro. He wants to stop because he's so tired but wants to make sure he nails his "interview."

"Sarah left some paperwork for you to fill out. But do it later," says Sam.

"Cutlery!" one of the wait staff yells into the kitchen.

The night flies by. A little after ten Ichiro finally removes his apron. He's damp and sweaty all over. His shoulders ache from pushing the racks around.

———.———

It's a short bus ride home. As he puts the key into the lock, he hears his mother's voice. Who is she talking to? "Mom, is someone here? Mom?" He hears the back patio door close. "Who was that, Mom?" he asks as he enters the kitchen.

"Just my boss," she says quickly. "He gave me a ride home." She doesn't sound like herself.

"Mom, are you okay?" Ichiro puts his arm around his mom's shoulders.

Her voice is very quiet. "Yes, I'm fine, Ichiro. I'm going to sleep now. Sorry, we can celebrate your birthday tomorrow. I'm so tired." She gives Ichiro a half hug and then turns away.

Chapter Three

The next morning, a Saturday, Ichiro wakes up to a text from Chris.

Hey, we're gonna hang out later with Lexie if you're free.

Sure.

Ichiro showers and fixes his hair with some gel wax. He puts on his favorite pair of boxer briefs, black jeans and his binder tank. Over those goes a white V-neck T-shirt and then a cool button-down shirt. Then he steps into his black leather boots. He checks the mirror and likes what he sees. He's looking forward to seeing Lexie again. She probably has a boyfriend already, he thinks, but she seems fun. It'd be nice to have a new friend.

"Going out, Mom," he calls. He doesn't know if she's home or not, but there's no response.

The coffee shop is close enough that he can walk there in five minutes. That's what he loves about living near Commercial Drive. When he arrives, he doesn't see his friends yet. He orders a matcha latte and a chocolate-chunk cookie.

Chris and Jia walk in with Lexie. "Hey!" they all say at the same time.

"Matcha latte!" the barista shouts. Ichiro picks up his order.

"Let's get our drinks and go to the park," Chris says.

"Good idea," says Jia. "It's too crowded in here."

Lexie goes up to the counter and orders a matcha latte too and a peanut butter cookie. "What kind of cookie did you get?" she asks Ichiro.

"Chocolate chunk," says Ichiro. He thinks it's cute that she also ordered a matcha latte and a cookie. Maybe it's a sign. Lexie smiles at him and stands close to him while she waits for her order.

When everyone has their coffee, they all head over to the park across the street.

Ichiro and Lexie walk together, ahead of Chris and Jia. Ichiro tries to make small talk.

"So where did you move here from?" he asks.

"Calgary," Lexie replies.

"What's it like there?"

"Flat and dry. Boring. My dad moved our family out here. Mom didn't want to come, but I was happy to. I had heard about how beautiful Vancouver is."

"Yeah, it sure is," says Ichiro. Lexie is walking really close to him now. But it's not making him feel uncomfortable at all. It feels right.

"But Ichiro, sometimes you say you hate this city," Jia pipes up. Chris just laughs. Ichiro blushes a bit and goes back to sipping his latte.

"Lexie's taking photography," Chris says.

"Cool. Do you have a camera?" Ichiro asks.

"A basic Canon digital SLR. My dad bought a used one for me."

"We should do photo walks together," Jia says.

"Who are your favorite photographers?" Ichiro asks.

"Claude Cahun, Man Ray, Cindy Sherman, Lee Miller and Vivian...what's her last name?"

"Maier," says Ichiro. He's impressed by the names she has listed. She's the real deal.

"Yes, that's it," Lexie says, smiling. "What about you? Who do you like?"

"Oh, um, Robert Frank, Walker Evans, Garry Winogrand, street photographers—"

"All men. What about women photographers?" Lexie asks.

Ichiro isn't sure if she's teasing him. "Uh...I like Mikiko Hara and Dorothea Lange—" he begins.

"Hey, let's sit here," Chris interrupts, pointing at a patch of grass.

"Lexie just broke up with her boyfriend," Jia says to Ichiro, a twinkle in her eye.

"Yeah," Lexie says, looking a little embarrassed. "He's in Calgary, so it's not like we were gonna see each other anytime soon."

"That sucks," says Ichiro. He hopes that sounded sincere enough.

"Well, maybe we will both find love soon," says Jia.

"First you have to figure out what you want!" Chris says, punching Jia lightly on the shoulder.

"That's not true. I want someone who is fun, smart and supportive. They have to be kind and like video games too."

"Video games?" asks Lexie.

"Yeah, I'm a bit of a gamer."

"Yeah," says Chris. "She likes to play *Sims 4* and *Stardew Valley*, so she thinks she's a gamer."

"Shut up!" Jia punches Chris hard on his shoulder.

"I *love Stardew Valley*," says Lexie. "What about you, Ichiro? Do you have a favorite game?"

"*Ghost of Tsushima*," says Ichiro. "It's PS5."

"Great choice," says Chris. "A fucking awesome game."

"Best game ever," says Ichiro. He realizes that he sounds a bit nerdy.

"Hey, Lexie, don't you live somewhere around here?" asks Jia.

"Down the street, right on the Drive. Above this Italian restaurant. It's kind of small for the three of us, but Dad says it'll have to do."

"I love Italian food," says Jia.

"It's nice, but it can be a bit noisy, especially when they turn on the live mic."

"Seriously?" says Chris.

"Yeah, the owner, Roger, likes to sing during some of their big events."

"I would love that," says Jia.

"It's cool, and they keep it quiet after eleven, so we can't really complain."

"Oh shit," says Jia, looking at her phone. "I missed a call from my mom."

"So what?" says Chris.

"She worries about me," says Jia. She looks like she's about to cry.

"Hey, Jia, I'm going to get ice cream. Do you want to come with?" asks Ichiro.

"Let's all go," says Lexie.

As they get up, Ichiro notices Chris checking out a couple of guys sitting nearby. Either of them could be his type. With his easygoing manner and talkative nature, he has no trouble getting boyfriends.

This time Ichiro walks with Jia. "Hey, Jia, is everything okay with you and your mom? I know it was rocky after you told her about your girlfriend."

"It took her a while to get used to us together, but eventually she was supportive. Then Mina and I broke up."

"Sorry about that."

"It's fine. It's for the best. Anyway, never got around to telling Dad. He still doesn't know."

They all order ice cream and sit down.

It's Ichiro's turn to be grilled. "Why don't we ever see you with anyone, Ichiro?" asks Jia.

Ichiro blushes. "Well, I—"

"Check that guy out," Chris interrupts. A young skater with short black hair, wearing a tank top that shows off his muscles, is fanning himself at the counter.

"OMG, Chris, calm down," says Jia. They all laugh.

"I'm into whoever," says Lexie.

"Yeah, I figured," says Chris. Lexie punches his arm. She glances at Ichiro.

Ichiro has realized he's really attracted to Lexie.

He doesn't like many people in that way, and when he does, it usually doesn't happen this fast.

"Ichiro, did you say something?" says Chris, smirking.

Jia kicks Chris under the table.

Ichiro chokes on his ice cream. "Oops, sorry. Some went down the wrong way."

Lexie laughs.

"So, Ichiro," says Jia. "I don't know if I've ever seen you with someone. Have you even kissed anyone before?" She laughs.

"Yeah," Ichiro mumbles. He wonders why Jia and Chris are being such jerks today.

"Really?" says Chris.

"Yeah, really?" says Jia. "Who?"

"Just someone I knew in ninth grade." Ichiro feels very uncomfortable now.

"We know all the same people, so who was it?" Chris will not leave it alone.

Now Lexie looks uncomfortable.

Ichiro takes his time with his Rocky Road cone. "Why does it matter to you guys?"

"*Folks*, not *guys*," says Jia. "I'm not a guy. Neither is Lexie."

"Okay, Jia. Ugh, sometimes you drive me nuts. I slipped. I know I should be using the more inclusive term. Believe me, I know."

Lexie tries changing the subject. "So what do you *folks* all do for fun?"

Ichiro smiles at her little dig at Jia.

Jia doesn't seem to notice. "Oh, we usually hang out in the park or over at my place. Sometimes we order pizza and watch Netflix. Chris and Ichiro play street hockey, like a couple of yahoos from the burbs. I love to read and hang out at the main library. I'm also working on a podcast about ghosts."

Jia is talking super fast. Sometimes Ichiro thinks she will never stop.

"Cool," says Lexie. "Are there lots of haunted places in Vancouver?"

"Tons," says Ichiro. "They even have some tours. Jia, Chris and I map out our own tours though. It's fun to do them on Halloween or on a Friday the thirteenth."

"Spooky," says Lexie.

"My favorite spots are in Gastown and down by the rail tracks on the waterfront," says Jia.

"WHOOOOooooooh!" says Chris, waving his arms like a ghost. "Jia loves the waterfront. There's a rumor that the ghost of a Chinese rail-yard worker hangs out on the tracks. She thinks they might be related somehow."

"Well, you never know," says Jia, pouting a little.

"Jia and the ghost have the same last name," Ichiro explains to Lexie.

"We should all go ghost hunting one night," suggests Lexie.

"In!" say Chris and Jia at the same time.

"If I'm not working," says Ichiro.

"You're always busy now," says Jia.

"I'm trying to save up."

"For what?" asks Chris.

"Just something," says Ichiro. Why are they so annoying today?

"Like a girlfriend?" Chris says in a singsong voice. Jia laughs.

"There *are* people I like, you know," says Ichiro.

"Yeah, who?" asks Chris.

"I'm just not sure if they would like me back," he replies. "You know. Because…" He trails off.

"What are you talking about?" asks Jia. "Why wouldn't they like you?"

"What do you mean, Ichiro?" Lexie asks.

"Just, well, I'm a bit different," says Ichiro. This is feeling really weird and awkward now.

"What does that even mean?" asks Jia. She almost sounds angry.

"Yeah, what are you really talking about?" Chris demands.

"There aren't many trans kids at school, and I feel so..." Ichiro looks down at his phone, not sure how to continue.

"*What*?" says Chris.

"Wait a second. Hold up," says Jia.

Ichiro is confused by his friends' confusion. But then he realizes he's never told Jia or Chris that he's trans. He just assumed they knew.

Chapter Four

"We had no idea!" says Jia. "Why didn't you ever tell us?"

"It's okay, it's cool," says Chris, "but yeah, we didn't know. I mean, we knew your pronouns, but…"

"I guess I never said anything specifically," says Ichiro. He feels *really* weird now and hopes they don't ask a lot of questions. He's not ready to answer them.

"Wow. But, yeah, it's fine," says Jia.

"Yeah," says Lexie.

"So are you doing hormone therapy?" asks Chris.

"No, nothing like that," Ichiro says as he looks out the window.

"Are you going to get surgery?" Jia asks. "Terry did and is super happy about his body shape."

"No, not right now," Ichiro says, looking at the floor now. He wishes they would just drop it.

"Shit, does your family know?"

"Not exactly."

"Oh," says Lexie. "Maybe they do know? But don't know how to talk to you about it?"

"Can we talk about something else?" Ichiro says.

"You've always been my brother anyway," says Chris. He punches Ichiro on the arm.

———.———

Ichiro frets about what happened all the way home. What if Chris and Jia blab to the other students?

Now that he realizes no one knew he was trans, he is nervous about it being "a thing."

"Mom?" No answer. Their home is in its usual state, quiet and empty. Ichiro goes upstairs, throws his stuff on the floor and lies on his bed for a bit, staring at the ceiling. He doesn't think Lexie will say anything because she's so new. She also doesn't seem like the type to talk about people's personal information. He loves Jia and Chris, but sometimes they talk too much. He can't believe his friends know he is trans. Does *he* even know for sure? And what about surgery and drugs? He doesn't know anymore.

He has a few long shifts at Café Ivy this week, so he won't be able to hang out with his friends as much. He feels relieved to have a bit of time away from that whole situation but also a bit sad, because he'll kind of miss seeing Lexie.

Time to focus. He's going to have to stay up late tonight and work on his history assignment. After a couple of hours, his eyeballs hurt and are starting to water. He closes up his laptop and crawls into bed. As he drifts off to sleep, he hears the sound of a car door slamming shut and then his mother at the front door. He looks over at his phone. It's 3:00 a.m. He turns over and tries to go back to sleep. But he hears something else. It's his mother, and she's crying. It sounds a bit muffled, but his door is open. Maybe he did fall back asleep and she came and checked on him earlier. He pulls on a shirt over his boxers and goes to his mom's room.

"Mom?"

"Ichiro, it's late. Go back to sleep."

"Are you okay?" He can see the outline of her figure sitting on the bed. She is definitely crying.

Ichiro moves forward and sits beside her on the bed. He puts his arm around her. She is visibly shaking.

"What's going on? Is it work?"

She doesn't reply.

"Mom! Tell me. Is something wrong? Is it your boss?"

She nods. "Ichiro," she says quietly. "Please, just leave it."

"No. I'm going down there first thing in the morning."

"Ichiro."

"I just want to talk to him."

"No, I don't want you to get involved."

"You can't let anyone do this to you. Did he say something to you, did he touch you?" Ichiro can't stand it. Who is this creep? "I'm going to tell him to leave you alone."

"He didn't touch me. He just…"

"What?"

"He says weird things, very odd—"

"Like, sexual things?"

She doesn't answer, just starts sobbing again.

"I don't want you to go back, Mom."

"I have to for now."

"No you don't."

"Ichiro, we have no money."

"I'm working now, and I'm going to take on more shifts. I can help."

"But our rent alone…"

"Mom, I'm going down there tomorrow to sort this out."

"No, Ichiro, not yet. I can't lose this job right now. Payday is next week, and we have to pay the rent for next month. Be patient. I'll figure this out."

———.———

Later Ichiro tries to get comfortable in bed, but his brain is on fire. He thinks about what his mother must be going through. He doesn't know what to do. This Friday will be his first payday, and he's calculated that he might get three hundred dollars after taxes if he's lucky. Definitely not enough to pay the rent. Neither of them has any savings either. He has to think of another way to help. The thought of anyone hurting his mother makes him so angry. He might have to go by her work tomorrow just to get a look at the guy.

A soft knock. His mother opens his door. She is acting calm and relaxed. But Ichiro knows it's only for his benefit. "I'll be okay, Ichiro. It was a busy day at work today, and I was feeling overwhelmed. See? I'm fine now. Get some rest for school tomorrow. Good night."

"Night, Mom," he says, but it's not over. He gets up and closes his door. Time for research. He looks up his mom's workplace to see if he can find any information on her boss. She hasn't been working there long, so there isn't much to go on other than his first name, Cliff. Nothing on the restaurant website shows anybody named Cliff. He looks at the Yelp reviews from customers. No mention of a Cliff. This guy must be a nobody. Ichiro's going to track him down and tell him to back off. He's so mad that he stops scrolling for a bit to do a round of push-ups to burn off some steam.

If only they could move somewhere cheaper. When he gets back on the computer, he starts looking around on Craigslist. He's heard a lot about tiny houses in the news, but do they have them in Vancouver ? How much do they cost? *Wait a second!* His eyes light up—he's got it!

Chapter Five

A few listings have caught his eye. What about a camper van? There are some older Westfalia models from the 1980s that might work. They're a bit shoddy, but they're in the right price range. Anything that old will need work, though, so it depends on how much money he can save. He'll calculate that after he gets his first paycheck. If he can figure out how to buy one, it could work. He's taking mechanics this term, and he heard about a shop project where the students choose a vehicle to all work on together. A run-down camper van could be the perfect fixer-upper!

It all sounds good, but Ichiro knows there's a lot about the world he doesn't know yet. Should he reach out to his dad? He doesn't even know where he is right now. He sends Ichiro a bit of money now and then. Ichiro feels weird asking him for anything though. Sometimes he wonders what it would have been like to have grown up with his dad. Maybe he could have traveled around with him while he took photos. It probably wouldn't have worked out—his dad was too attached to his freedom.

Ichiro could ask for more shifts at the café. But then he wouldn't be able to see his friends much or get to know Lexie better. Maybe he could sell some of his things. He looks around his room. His hockey-card collection? He could get some of his old rookie cards appraised. He's been collecting for a long time and knows some of the cards he has are worth something. Even if he only gets a couple hundred dollars, every little bit helps.

He eventually falls asleep, his dreams full of budgets and dollar signs. His alarm clock goes off. It reads *8:45*. He's late again! It must have gone off earlier and Ichiro hit *snooze*, but he can't remember. He throws his laptop and supplies into his backpack, hops onto his skateboard and heads to school. *Oh crap.* He's forgotten to text his mother to let her know he's okay and heading to school. She's already at work, because her Fridays are always super busy. He can't even remember what class he should be going to. *Oh shit, it's calculus.* Mr. Turner is a real stickler about students being on time. Ichiro picks up his pace. As he enters the school grounds, he trips on the pavement. He can see himself falling in slow motion but is unable to stop. He puts his hands out to brace his fall and ends up scraping his palms on the gravel.

He goes through the doors and heads straight to the bathroom to wash off the blood. Mr. Turner will be upset that he's late again.

Ichiro approaches the back door of the classroom. Through the window he can see that Mr. Turner has his back turned, facing the whiteboard. Ichiro slowly turns the metal doorknob with both hands and slips in. The kids in the back turn their heads and try not to giggle. Ichiro grabs an empty chair and quietly sets his backpack on the floor. He wipes sweat from his brow. The student beside him gives him a *what's up?* look. They bump elbows.

Mr. Turner drones on. "So if *f* is a function whose graph is the parabola shown here, then *f(x)* < 0 whenever…" He writes on the whiteboard:

$x < 1$ or $x > 3$

or $x < 1$

or $x > 3$

or $1 < x < 3$?

"Does anyone know the answer or want to take a guess?" Mr. Turner asks as he turns around to face the class. "Did everyone do the exercises I assigned to you last week?"

"Is it $x < 1$?" a student asks.

"Yes, that is correct. Great work, Stephanie."

Ichiro starts to relax. Maybe he got away with it. He grabs his water from his backpack and takes a big swig.

"Ichiro, please come see me after class," says Mr. Turner.

Crap.

A few of the students snort. Ichiro puts his head down and opens up his laptop to start going over last week's homework.

"Let's move on to another question." Mr. Turner starts talking about the standard coordinate system.

"When are we ever going to use this stuff anyway?" whispers a student sitting close to Ichiro.

His name is Tom. Tom is busy looking at his phone and playing a game hidden just behind his backpack.

Ichiro ignores him. He is thinking about how he doesn't want to meet with Mr. Turner after class today of all days. He's supposed to meet up with his friends for lunch. He hasn't seen them in over a week. He's really hoping that Lexie will be there too.

When the class ends, Ichiro starts packing up his stuff. Maybe the teacher has forgotten that he wants to talk to him. He slings his backpack on and moves toward the door.

"Ichiro, do you have a few minutes?"

"Yes, Mr. Turner." There is no escape.

"Ichiro, is everything okay? You didn't hand in the first assignment of the term. It's only worth 10 percent of your final mark, but this isn't like you. What's going on? You were also late again today. That is very disruptive to the other students."

"I know, sorry," says Ichiro. "I've got a lot going on. But I'm going to get caught up on the exercises this week. I promise."

"And don't think I didn't notice you closing your eyes either. Are you having trouble sleeping? There are counselors available for you to talk to if you need them."

"No, I'm just really busy."

"Well, you're going to have to figure out a way to make time for your schoolwork. It's important."

"Okay. I get it. Thanks."

"Get outta here then and enjoy your afternoon."

As Ichiro leaves the classroom, he sees Lexie passing by. But she has her arms linked with some guy he doesn't recognize. Ichiro's heart sinks a bit. Now he wants to go somewhere and hide. If only he'd been quicker at asking her out for real.

Chapter Six

Where r u?

That's Chris.

On my way.

Hurry up. I'm starving and we want to eat.

That's Jia.

Two minutes.

Ichiro goes straight to the cafeteria and sees Jia and Chris. They wave him over. *Ugh*. Right beside them is Lexie with that guy. They seem to be sitting really close as they chat and laugh.

"Hey," says Ichiro. He tries not to look Lexie's way.

"Let's get some food. Do we want to eat here or go to the diner?" Chris asks.

"Diner might be busy. Let's eat here," Ichiro says. "I have to leave a bit early."

"Oh, this is Virat," says Lexie. "Virat, this is Ichiro."

Ichiro is forced to look at Virat. He is handsome and quite stylish.

"Hey," says Virat, "nice to meet you. It's cool to hang with you all." He moves closer to Lexie, and Ichiro feels a bit uneasy.

"So, Virat, what's your story?" asks Jia.

"Moved here a couple of weeks ago. Lexie and I both have friends who live in that new housing complex down in Meadow Grove."

"Cool."

"Yeah, cool," Ichiro says, trying to smile. "Well, I'm going to grab some food."

"I'll come with you," says Lexie.

"Me too," says Jia. "You were taking forever, Ichiro."

"Yeah, sorry. Turner wanted to talk to me."

"You in trouble? You never get into trouble," Jia says.

"Oh, really?" says Lexie, laughing a little.

What did *that* mean? "Yeah, well, I've been busy working and stuff. I haven't been keeping up. Plus I was late today."

"But you're never late," Jia says.

"No, but in the last few weeks I've missed my alarm a few times. I'm doing lots of shifts at work," says Ichiro.

"Why are you working so much?" asks Jia.

"Well…" Ichiro looks away. He doesn't really want to get into it.

"Maybe he has a good reason," says Lexie. "If you need summaries for classes, I have some notes from my teacher. Most of the material is the same."

"Thanks, Lexie," says Ichiro.

"So what's the deal with you and Virat?" Jia asks Lexie. "He's kinda cute." Ichiro is glad she asked, but he moves out of the way and orders his lunch. He knows Jia will fill him in later if necessary.

"Oh, we're just friends. He's looking for a boyfriend," Lexie says.

Ichiro hears this and his heart starts racing. Maybe he has a chance after all.

"Cool. Might not take him long," says Jia. "After all, we did leave him with Chris." She laughs, and all three of them look over at the table. Virat and Chris are deep in discussion. They look like they are having fun.

"Awesome," says Lexie. She moves closer to Ichiro.

Ichiro decides to go for it. "Hey, um, Lexie, do you want to hang out sometime?" he asks quietly as he grabs a plate from the cafeteria. "If you have time," he adds.

"If I have time? Don't you mean if *you* have time?"

Ichiro pulls out his phone. "What's your IG?"

Lexie tells him her handle, which includes her last name.

"Kushi?" Ichiro says as he types her information into his phone. "So you're Japanese too. My last name is Ito."

Lexie's phone pings. She adds him back right away. "Oh, that's kinda cool," she replies. "Ichiro Ito. I love alliteration."

"Fuck, you two! Hurry up so we can eat," says Jia. They get their food and go back to their table. Chris and Virat stand up to go get some food. Ichiro moves over closer to Lexie.

"So here's a conversation starter," says Lexie. "What kinds of books do you like to read?"

"I'm into horror fiction, things like *Anna Dressed in Blood*," says Jia. "Or *The Forest of Hands and Teeth*," she adds.

"Oh, I love those books too," says Lexie.

Ichiro keeps eating, hoping Lexie doesn't ask him.

"What about you?" Lexie asks Ichiro.

"I, uh, I like to read a lot of nonfiction."

"Boooooooriing," says Jia.

"Shut up, Jia," Ichiro says. But he's smiling.

"Oh, that's kinda cool," says Lexie. "What are you reading right now?"

"bell hooks." Ichiro feels like a dweeb saying it.

"Nice. I love her stuff. I really like *All About Love*," says Lexie.

Ichiro blushes. "Uh, yeah. I'm reading her *Writing Beyond Race* right now."

"That one too," says Lexie.

Ichiro can't believe it. Lexie is so cool.

"Lexie, what are you reading?" asks Jia.

"A couple of really interesting art books. One is about Lee Ufan, and the other's about Yoshitomo Nara." Ichiro nods his head. Lexie notices. "So you know who I'm talking about then?"

"Yeah, I like their work too," he says.

Chris and Virat return. "Hey, what'd you all get to eat?" Chris asks. "By the time we got up there, they only had pasta with plain tomato sauce and garlic bread left."

"Burgers and fries, the lunch of kings and queens," says Jia.

"What the fuck. I'm blaming Ichiro. Next time, get here quicker, bud," says Chris.

Ichiro throws a fry at Chris, who picks it up off the table and eats it.

"So, Virat, what's your type?" Chris asks.

"No type. I'm just into whoever I'm attracted to."

"Right," says Chris. "So am *I* your type then?" He flutters his eyelashes.

"Oh sure, honey," says Virat and caresses Chris's cheek.

They all laugh because Chris's face is bright red. They've never seen him blush.

"So, Lexie, you're Japanese?" asks Jia.

"Half. Mom's Japanese and Dad's Chinese."

"Wow, same as Ichiro," says Jia.

"What about you, Virat?"

"Indian. Mom is from Mumbai, and Dad is from Chennai. We were living in Chennai before moving here for Dad's work. He's an engineer, and Mom's a teacher."

"My parents are Chinese. From Hong Kong," says Jia.

"Mine are from the Philippines," says Chris. "Gang, we are from all over. Internationals represent!"

"I'm glad I found you all. It's hard to find a place to fit in," says Lexie.

"I know what you're saying. I don't fit in with the Japanese group or the Chinese group, 'cause I'm sort of in this in-between space," Ichiro says.

"Good thing you have us," says Jia.

Ichiro's phone buzzes. It's Sarah from Café Ivy.

We really need help tonight. What time can you get here?

"Shit, I have to work," says Ichiro. "Thought I'd finally get an evening off."

"We'll bring you late-night snacks at the end of your shift," says Jia.

"Yeah, it's Friday night, bud," says Chris.

"I'm in!" says Lexie.

"Hey, Virat, do you want to join us tonight?" Chris asks.

"Meet you all there. I just need to check in with my parents," says Virat.

"One o'clock, peeps. Back to class."

Lexie squeezes Ichiro's elbow and gives him a smile. "See you tonight."

Chapter Seven

"Thanks for coming in. I'm Sarah. Nice to finally meet you in person. Sorry it's so last minute. Lots of shifts coming up, and you've been so reliable. Have a look and let me know what you want, okay?"

"Awesome! Thanks. I need as many shifts as I can get right now."

"Ichiro's saving up for a camper van for his mom," says Sam. He throws Ichiro some clean towels.

"Use these for cleaning up. Unload those racks too. We're running out of space."

The plates coming out of the dishwasher are always so hot. It's the part Ichiro hates the most. The steam makes him sweat and his hair falls flat. If only he could rush home to have a quick shower and put on a fresh set of clothes. Sam is busy prepping the vegetables, and Ichiro watches because he's so quick with his hands. Sarah said that soon Ichiro will get to do some prep work.

"You look nervous. What's going on?" says Sam.

"Oh, some friends are coming by later, that's all."

"One must be really cute," says Sam, clicking his tongue.

"Wish I had a change of clothes. You know how I look after a shift."

"You can borrow the spare shirt I keep in my locker. I'm too tired to go out later."

"Sweet, thanks! Uh, Sam, do you know of any other places hiring? I need extra cash."

"How much more can you do, friend?"

"I know, but I need to get that camper van so my mom will be safe."

"What's going on?"

"Some dude at her work is harassing her. Her boss."

"Oh, harsh!"

"Yeah. She doesn't want to lose her job, so she can't say anything right now."

"Hey, you two, more work, less chat. Dishes are piling up."

"Sorry, sorry," says Ichiro. He can't believe there is so much grease on everything. He tries to pre-soak some of the messier pans in the tub first, but everything still feels slick and slippery. Earlier he almost slipped on the floor tiles. He feels so nervous about meeting up with Lexie later tonight. What if he says the wrong thing or, worse, doesn't have much to say at all? Sometimes he can be like that. He's trying to relax, but it's so busy tonight, and he still has homework for Turner's class too. It'll be another sleepless night.

"What's your plan for the camper van?" asks Sam.

"Get an older model and fix it up in the shop at school. Every year they take on one larger project and everyone works on it. Some grads come in and help out too. I just need to convince them to use the camper van."

"Cool, but that's gonna be a lot of work."

"Yeah, for sure. I'm trying to get the best with whatever I can save."

"How are you going to get that much money?"

"I told my aunt what's going on. She's going to co-sign a loan for me. But I have to come up with a couple thousand dollars by the end of summer. Then I'll pay the rest of it back over the next few years."

"Okay, buddy, best of luck. I have a friend who works at the gay club on Main Street. They have these youth drag nights with some decent prize money to encourage kids to get into drag. You ever thought about doing something like that?"

"I guess, but nothing serious."

"If you're interested go talk to my friend Mike at the Sidecar and ask him about it."

"Great. Thanks, I'll check it out."

"Or maybe he needs some other kind of help. They are always busy," he adds.

The plates are starting to pile up again, and Ichiro needs to move faster. He's carefully loading in the glassware. He can't break any more tonight. He's in machine mode, and it seems like he's been washing and cleaning forever. Finally he can see that the customers are thinning out.

At around ten o'clock one of the servers comes to the back. "Your friends are here, Ichiro. Are you almost done?"

"Yeah, just need to run a few more racks through after the staff have finished eating."

"Go see your friends. You can do those later," says Sam. "And see what your friends want to eat. I can make it for you and your friends."

"Seriously?"

"Yeah, just the basics, as the kitchen is more or less closed right now. But I can whip up the easier things on the grill."

Ichiro goes out and grabs the seat next to Lexie in the booth. "Hey, all!"

"How's it going?" asks Chris.

"So tired. But we can order stuff from the grill, and they'll make it for us on the house."

"So cool," says Lexie.

Sam comes over and pretends to be the waiter. "Your choice of burgers, fish and chips, or grilled cheese, with sodas or iced tea."

"Thanks, Sam."

Sam winks at Ichiro.

"What are you all up to on the weekend?" says Lexie.

"Hike with Virat," says Chris.

"Where to?" asks Lexie.

"Grouse Mountain. You can come with us if you want, Lex."

"Nah, I'll leave you boys alone. Where is Virat anyway?"

"His parents wanted him home tonight."

"I'm planning to go thrift-store shopping," says Jia.

"Can I come with?" Lexie asks.

"Yeah, let's head out early so everything isn't so picked over. The Value Thrift near my place is the best."

"Do you wanna come, Ichiro?" asks Lexie.

"As long as it's before my shift starts. I do need an outfit." He's thinking about the club.

Chris laughs. "Yeah, for dates and things."

"Shut up," says Ichiro, giving Chris a sideways middle finger. Their food comes, and Lexie places her hand on Ichiro's right knee and leaves it there for what feels like forever.

Ichiro's thoughts are all over the place. He's happy that Lexie seems interested but is still thinking about what Sam said about his friend's club. Could he actually do drag? Sure, he has tried on his mother's clothes and played around with her makeup. He's also practiced lip-syncing, but how does he do the rest?

Chapter Eight

"Morning, Mom."

"Good morning. I have to head off to work in a few minutes—where are my keys?!"

"Listen, Mom. I have an idea. I want to buy us a camper van. That way we don't have to—"

"Help me find my keys, Ichiro."

"After I graduate we can live on the Island, on Auntie Edna's property—Mom, are you listening?"

"We have just enough money for groceries, okay?" Ichiro's mom pushes a twenty-dollar bill his way. "Can you pick up some milk, bread, soy sauce, veggies and fruit?"

"I'll get it this time. Keep your money."

"Save your money for school. I can't pay for university. You know that."

"I know, but I can buy groceries sometimes. I'm working a lot now."

"Okay, honey."

"Mom, what about my plan?"

"Let's talk another time. I have enough for rent this month. Where are my keys? Did you—"

"I can fix up a camper van for us."

"Insurance, gasoline and repairs cost money too. Plus I don't think it's a good idea to live with Auntie Edna."

"I asked her," he says.

"You what?"

"She said it would be fine."

"Ichiro, I don't need handouts from my sister."

"Just until we get better jobs. Maybe I could go to school on the Island."

"I can't talk about this right now. Help me find my keys. I'm going to be late."

"I have work at the café, and I'm going to make extra money with banquets and—"

"Ichiro, please! I have to go right now. If you're not going to help me find my keys, then go do something else. Your room is a mess." She looks in the fridge for her keys.

"No it's not. It's disorganized because I'm so busy."

"Your clothes are all over. There are empty bubble-tea containers everywhere."

"Do you think my plan will work? I just want to get started."

She finds the keys in one of the pockets of a jacket on the couch. "I have to go now. We'll talk about this another time." She slams the door on her way out.

She seems really angry. Ichiro thinks it must be because she doesn't really get along with her sister. They used to fight a lot as kids.

Ichiro downs a glass of orange juice before heading out to meet Jia and Lexie at the thrift store.

———.———

Jia is waiting outside Value Thrift. Ichiro locks up his bike and walks over. "Hey, Jia!"

"Lexie just texted. She's on her way. Why are you here, Ichiro? Can't stay away from Lexie?" She laughs.

"Ha ha. Picking up a few things for Mom. Besides, I was invited."

"That's sweet," says Jia just as Lexie arrives.

"Sorry I'm a bit late. Let's have some fun!" Lexie loops her arms into Ichiro's and Jia's and leads them into the store. The girls head toward the sweaters and start looking through the racks.

Ichiro finds a rack labeled *costumes* and picks up a hot-pink jumpsuit. Would this work for drag? He looks around and then heads toward the mirror. He holds it up against his chest and looks at his reflection. *Not bad.* A couple of older women start to giggle. He ignores them. He moves the sleeves up and down and tries to imagine himself wearing this onstage. It needs something more. He grabs a curly blue wig from a nearby stand and loosely places it on his head. *Hmmm.* He could get used to this. He doesn't look half-bad. He looks at the price tag. It's just $15 for the jumpsuit, but the wig is $35. Plus he'd still need to buy makeup and do something about his shoes. He looks again at his reflection and knows he will figure out a way. He twirls around and sees Jia and Lexie watching him. They look puzzled.

"What are you doing, Ichiro?" asks Jia. "Is that something for Halloween? Because I don't think your mom would wear that." Lexie just giggles.

Ichiro's face goes red, and he throws the jumpsuit and wig on the floor. "I thought it was funny. Just playing around, waiting for you two."

"Look what we found." Jia holds up a bulky, light-gray cardigan. "It's so cool—it has pockets and a hood. Looks like it's from the seventies. It will go nicely over a cool button-down."

"What'd you find, Lexie?" Ichiro asks.

She holds up a knitted leaf-lace halter top in a light mauve. "I'm gonna try it on. Can you both come with me? I don't know if the look is right for me or not."

"Sure," says Jia. Ichiro shifts around, keeping his eye on the items he tossed on the floor.

"What's wrong with you?" Jia says when Lexie goes into one of the narrow changerooms.

"Nothing," says Ichiro.

"You need to loosen up, man. This is supposed to be fun!"

"Yeah, I know. I'm a bit stressed."

"Yeah, I get it," says Jia. "But if you like Lexie, you're going to have to chill out. Lexie is super cool, and a couple of other people at school have already asked her out."

She pushes Ichiro toward the changeroom. "Get in there!"

"Yikes, not that close, Jia!" says Ichiro.

Jia laughs.

Lexie comes out of the changeroom. The halter top looks great on her—but Ichiro is shocked by how see-through it is. "I guess I should wear a tank underneath," she says.

Ichiro doesn't say anything.

"I love it," says Jia. "You look hot."

"What do you think, Ichiro?"

"Uh, it's nice," he says. "It makes you look great. Or, I mean, you make it look great."

"Oh my god," Jia says. Lexie just laughs.

Ichiro's phone buzzes. A text from his mom.

Sorry about earlier. Talk later? I have some news.

Ichiro wonders what that could be about. He notices the time.

"I have to get to work," he says. "This was fun. Thanks. See you later."

"What about this?" Jia asks, holding up the pink jumpsuit and blue wig.

Ichiro runs out of the store.

Chapter Nine

When Ichiro gets home after his shift, the lights aren't on. That means his mother is still not home. She puts on every light she can when she's home alone. It's after eleven. She's not usually this late. Ichiro is looking forward to relaxing a bit. His shift tomorrow doesn't start until five in the afternoon. He's got homework to do, but he's going to play some video games until his mom gets home. He wonders again what she wants to tell him. He hopes his grandpa is okay. Mom hasn't mentioned his grandparents recently.

He throws his stuff on his bed. Instead of playing video games, he decides to go into his mother's room. He looks at all the lipsticks lined up on her vanity table. He picks one that doesn't look like it gets used much—she might not notice it's missing. He goes back to his room and locks the door. Standing in front of the mirror, he applies it carefully to see how it looks. *Not bad.* He looks up some drag tutorials on YouTube. *Wow, there is so much to learn! So many different kinds of makeup!* He's going to start out with the basics. Then there are the outfits. He won't need to worry about padding, at least. He's also glad he doesn't have to tuck any balls. It all sounds difficult. He's a quick learner though. He will probably need a wig too. This is going to cost him some of his savings for the camper van. He starts practicing his dance routine and lip-syncing. It's tough going. He's just a baby drag queen. He needs a lot of help.

He checks his email. His first check from the café has come in. He looks at the pay stub. A lot has been taken off for taxes. The total is not as much as he was hoping for, especially for all that work. He sits on the edge of his bed and covers his face with his hands. He needs to think about how he's going to be able to do this. His shifts at the café and some banquets at school are helping a bit. But he might not have enough in a few months for the down payment. He's starting to feel desperate. He decides to talk to Sam's friend and see if there is other work he can do at the club on the youth nights.

He hears his mom's keys in the door.

"Mom, you're so late!"

She comes over to give Ichiro a hug. Then she takes off her jacket and collapses on the couch. She pats the cushion beside her.

"Come, sit. Let's talk about that vehicle—what's it called?"

"A camper van," says Ichiro. "We buy one and move to the Island. I have money saved up."

"Show me what you mean," she says.

Ichiro goes and grabs his laptop. "It's small, but we'd only use it for sleeping. There are campgrounds with showers if we move around. This one comes with a portable toilet and sink."

"Too small," she says.

"But think of the freedom. You can quit your job and look for something else while I work and go to uni."

"No, Ichiro. You should be enjoying life with your friends…" She trails off as she stares at him. "What's on…? Are you wearing *lipstick*?"

Ichiro realizes too late that he has forgotten to take it off.

"Yes, Mom. It's for a show. I'm thinking of doing drag. There's a club that—"

"Drag? A club? What do you mean? No daughter of mine is going to a place like that." She makes a funny, sour face and shakes her head.

"Mom, I'm trans." Ichiro feels like he might die.

"What does that mean?" She sounds angry.

"For me, it means I'm not your daughter. I'm your child, but I am not a girl."

"Ichiro, what are you saying? Why are you making my life difficult right now? I can't take this."

"At this youth club, I can make some extra money. I—"

"You will *not* be going to that club."

"It's not a big deal. It's work." He shrugs his shoulders.

"Well then, I'm going to start dating my boss. It's what he wants. And it will make our lives easier."

"No, Mom!" He's glaring at her.

"Yes, I have to. Only for now. He's not that bad. I'll find another job soon."

"Just wait, please. I'll have enough money for a down payment soon. Auntie Edna said—"

"Stop. I don't want to hear any more about her."

"She's going to help, so that we can—"

"Stop it right now!" she yells.

But he can't give up. "You have to let me do this. Let me help you!"

"No. You stop now." She sounds as if she is going to cry.

"I'm going to go to the club and see what Sam's friend has to say."

"You will not go to the club, Ichiro."

This is going nowhere. Ichiro stomps to his room and slams his door. He is old enough to make his own choices. Although he's always listened to his mother, now he has no choice but to defy her.

He can hear her standing outside his door. Ichiro starts playing a video game. He won't be sleeping or doing any homework tonight. His mother bangs on his door and tries to open it. She's never been this mad before. He can hear her sobbing outside his door, but he can't open it tonight. After a few minutes she finally leaves.

Chapter Ten

Ichiro goes to the club right after work. It's on Main Street and not far away from his apartment by bike. He's been by before but never inside. It's quiet, too early for a line to be forming outside. He's often seen one snaking around the block later in the day. Inside is empty, although Ichiro can hear lots of prep noises coming from the kitchen. He heads for that door and peers inside.

"Hey, I'm looking for Mike," Ichiro says to one of the staff chopping vegetables at lightning speed.

"Mike? Yeah, he should be here soon," they reply. "May I ask why you're looking for Mike?"

"My friend Sam said to come see him about maybe getting some work."

"Oh, cool. We always need extra help. I'll mention it when he comes in. What's your name?"

"Ichiro."

"Daveed." He gives Ichiro a nod. "Do you have any kitchen experience?"

"Yeah, I work at a café and help out in the cafeteria. I've done banquets too."

"Cool. Mike shouldn't be long," Daveed says. "You can grab a seat out in the dining room."

Ichiro sits down at a high bar table. There are spotlights pointing toward a small stage upfront. Just then a group of drag queens comes in from a door near the stage. They head straight for Ichiro.

"Oh, look, we have an audience of one already," one says.

Ichiro blushes.

"Hi, honey," another says. "Boy, you're cute."

"Jesus, Marky, he looks pretty young," the tallest one scolds.

"What are you doing here?" says the first one.

Ichiro has noticed she is wearing high-tops.

"I'm...uh...waiting for Mike," says Ichiro.

"Mike? Why would anyone wait for Mike?" They all burst out laughing.

"How do we look tonight, sweetheart?"

"Beautiful," Ichiro says. He likes how they're including him, but he feels a bit awkward.

"You have the perfect baby drag face, Ichiro. Let us know if you want us to help you out," says the tall one. "There's a youth drag night here, and they offer some great prize money. You should consider entering. My name is Lana, by the way." She twirls her long blond ponytail. Ichiro wonders how she can walk in her extremely high heels. Ichiro blushes as Lana leans in closer. "Oh honey, don't be shy," she teases.

"I-I…" Ichiro wants to say something, but the words are not coming out.

"Seriously, let me know if you want some help. Our drag family has room for you."

"Lana, leave them alone," one of the other queens with perfectly styled long black hair says.

"Yeah, you're going to scare them away. They aren't here to see you, they want to see Mike."

Lana puts on a pouty face. "Bye, sweetie," she says as the group heads to the bar. They grab some drinks and then all head back behind the stage. That must be where the changerooms are, thinks Ichiro.

He looks around. It seems like a decent hangout. He doesn't know why he hasn't been to a youth night here before.

He gets a text message from his mom.

Ichiro, I'm sorry. Are you okay?

Yes, Mom, I'm fine. I'm sorry too.

Okay, see you tonight.

She would be so upset if she knew he was here. He's glad she didn't ask, because he's not a very good liar.

"Yo, I heard you were waiting for me?" Mike has just come into the club. He's wearing a green tank top and a pair of tight shorts that show off his muscular thighs. He must do CrossFit, thinks Ichiro.

"Oh hey, Sam said to talk to you about some work."

"We need help in the kitchen, but the shifts start pretty late because we close at two a.m. Will that be a problem?" Mike asks.

"I could stay until one a.m. Would that be okay?" Ichiro asks.

"For sure. We're desperate. Sam said you have done some dishwashing, that right?"

"Yeah, but I also work in our school's cafeteria doing some prep work too."

"Fantastic. We just have small bites here, so we can probably train you up quick. You have your Food Safe?"

"Yeah, they made us get it at school."

"Guess with school you are available for evening shifts only?"

"I can do weekends too."

"What, no friends?"

"I have friends. But I need the money."

"Watch you don't burn yourself out. I used to do that, and I regret not spending more time having fun. You're only young once." Mike extends his hand to Ichiro. "I'll be in touch about some shifts soon," he says with a handshake.

———·———

Ichiro sneaks into the house quietly. He's not sure if his mom is home yet. Her schedule is all over the place. He's exhausted and not in the mood for talking or fighting tonight. He hopes to put in a couple of hours on homework before passing out. He grabs his phone and sets a series of three alarms for the morning, each five minutes apart. He's having trouble pulling himself out of bed. It's such a struggle to get to school on time now that he's so busy. Math homework, calculus—ugh, this is the worst. He tries solving a few of the exercises and equations. He makes good progress on them and loses track of time. A noise outside breaks his concentration.

There are two people shouting outside, but he can't quite make out what they are saying. He heads for the front door and realizes one of the people is his mother. He runs outside. "Mom, are you okay?"

"Ichiro, go back inside the house."

Ichiro realizes the other person must be Cliff. He's a big guy around fifty with sandy-blond hair. Looks like a bully and a loser. He has a big scar above his left eyebrow and is wearing a Bulls jersey. "Hey there, how are you tonight?" he says to Ichiro in a fake-friendly voice. "Your mom and I are just talking."

"You should leave her alone," says Ichiro.

"Ichiro!"

"Don't worry, son."

"Don't call me 'son.'" Ichiro is ready to hit this guy.

"Of course. I didn't mean anything by it," says Cliff.

"Ichiro, please go inside the house. I will be right there. *Now*, please," his mother says, raising her voice.

"Okay, but I'm at the door if you need anything." Ichiro gives his biggest scowl to Cliff.

There's more shouting, and he peers through the blinds. *What a jerk.* A car door slams shut hard, and tires squeal. *What an immature asshole.* His mom is fiddling with the door handle. It keeps turning right and left, left and right, like she doesn't remember how to open their front door. Ichiro opens it up for her.

She is crying.

"Mom, what happened? Oh my god, tell me."

Chapter Eleven

"I told him I quit because I can't take it anymore. He makes me feel uncomfortable, he keeps pressuring me, and he's so sneaky about it. I don't have witnesses because he bugs me when no one else is around. I don't know what to do anymore. I'm so sorry. I don't know why I thought I could go out with him. I can't." She is crying and talking, and Ichiro can barely make out what she is saying.

"Don't worry, Mom. I have a job, and I am saving. The camper van idea—doesn't it look like a better option now?"

"I don't have enough for rent next month, Ichiro!" she blurts out.

"It's okay. I almost have enough for us to get away from this city soon. We can live with Auntie Edna. There is enough room in their backyard for a camper van. It won't be long until I graduate."

"I'm going to look for another job tomorrow."

"Don't worry. It will all work out."

"Ichiro, maybe we should move back to Japan and stay with your grandparents. Then I can look after my mom and dad."

"No, we can't do that." Ichiro is being selfish. He can't imagine living in Japan. He wants to visit, but from what he's heard, it's way too strict of a country.

"Let's talk tomorrow. You need to get to sleep. And I have a big day of job hunting ahead of me."

"Really, Mom, I can help." Ichiro wonders if he can though.

———.———

The next morning he wakes up more determined than ever to earn as much money as possible in his final year of high school. He wants to start a new life somewhere else. Mike texts him about shifts at the club. Most of them are late-night shifts, but he tells Ichiro he'll adjust them so his shifts end at one a.m. at the latest.

Ichiro is at the library, printing out the forms Mike sent to him, when Lexie walks in. She's checking out a large stack of paperbacks.

"Hey, Lexie!" Ichiro is really happy to see her.

"Hi! What's up?"

"I'm using the printer. I have some shifts at a late-night kitchen."

"I don't know how you can do all that you do."

"I'm saving for a camper van." He picks up his forms from the printer.

"Why a camper van?" She places her books on the self-checkout scanner.

"For my mom. So we won't have to pay so much rent. Maybe just a pad fee and maintenance."

"Sweet. My cousin is selling a kind of camper thing, not sure what it is, but I can check, if you like," Lexie says.

"Thanks, but I think I'm good." He starts packing up to leave for class. "Are you getting used to the city now?" he asks.

"Yeah, I love it here. Hey, can you recommend a good gelato shop? I know the one with six hundred flavors that everyone talks about, but I want someplace a little less crowded."

"Oh, you gotta try Elephant Garden Creamery on the Drive. They have Asian-inspired flavors like Hong Kong Milk Tea, Mango Coconut Sticky Rice and Lemon Yuzu Butter. I love that place."

"It sounds perfect," she says. She fiddles with her long hair and places her stack of books in the bag. It looks like there are a couple of video games in the pile too, but Ichiro can't make out which ones they are.

"Do you want to go together? How about Sunday afternoon?" He thinks he sounded chill as he asked, but he's never sure.

"Okay, I'm in."

When Ichiro gets to English class, he realizes he only has about ten minutes to do some speed reading. Enough time to skim the questions for discussion. He needs to concentrate. He's in the zone when Chris sits down next to him.

"Hey, buddy, what's up? Lexie says you guys are going for gelato on Sunday."

"Yup," he says, keeping his head down.

"Cool. I haven't been to that place. She mentioned Elephant something?"

He wishes Chris would get the message. He marks

down a few notes and comments that might sound intelligent in case the teacher calls on him.

"Did the shop teacher email you yet? I was talking to him, and it sounds like he's cool with your camper van project," Chris says.

"What? Are you serious?"

"Yeah, I gave you props, told him the deal with your mom and you."

Sometimes Chris talks too much, but this is one of the times Ichiro is happy to have such a good friend. "Chris, buddy, that is amazing. Thanks."

"No prob. He's going to get in touch. So you better start figuring out how to get that camper van soon."

Now Ichiro can't concentrate at all. He just wants the school day to be over.

Chapter Twelve

Ichiro goes straight to the club after his shift at the café and realizes that this schedule is going to take some getting used to. Almost every hour of his day is busy with school or work. He's looking forward to the little bit of time he'll get to spend with Lexie on Sunday. Hopefully Chris won't crash the party.

"Ichiro!" says Mike. "Come on over here. I want to introduce you to the kitchen staff working today.

This is Nancy—she's the head cook here—and this is Angelo. He's the line cook. Angelo is going to show you the ropes for prep. We will need you to help out with dishes too 'cause we're short-staffed."

"Sure. No problem," Ichiro says.

"Hey, Ichiro," says Angelo. He is in his early twenties and has a gentle charm about him. "I'm going to get you started with vegetables, okay?"

"Sounds good. Hey, Mike, do you know the drag performer Lana?"

"Why, is she bothering you?" asks Mike.

"No, no. I wanted to ask her to show me some drag stuff."

"Oh, she's great at that. Like I said, that youth contest, the next one, is sponsored. Some serious money up for grabs," he says. "Do you have her contact info?"

"Yeah, she gave it to me when we first met," Ichiro replies.

"She moves fast, that one," says Angelo. Nancy and Mike laugh.

"Okay, Ichiro, you get going on cutting up some veggies," says Nancy. "Check out what's in the fridge. Give them a good wash. Let's see your knife skills. Then fill each of these buckets with the different veg types."

The club is open now, and Ichiro can sense the excitement in the air. The hum of the crowd and the glow from the flashing lights hits the kitchen as the door swings open. It's Lana.

"Hi, honeys. How are my favorite cooks doing?"

"Hey, Lana, can I ask you something?" says Ichiro.

She sashays over in her impressive heels. "Make it quick, honey. I have to go onstage in a few minutes."

"That's what *he* said," says Angelo, waggling his eyebrows. Mike and Nancy laugh.

"Can you, uh, maybe help me out with some drag stuff?"

"You're going to take me up on my offer?" she says. "Excellent. Text me a time that works for you." She's already out the door.

"What kind of persona are you going to take on?" Angelo asks.

"No idea," says Ichiro. He's going to have to think about this.

The music inside the club is getting louder. It sounds like the DJ has taken the stage. When he's on a break, Ichiro gets a text from Lexie.

Hey, my cousin has something called an A-liner. It's a mini trailer, but it's cool.

Never heard of those.

He says it's more affordable than a Westfalia camper van. You can rent a vehicle to drive it to where you want to go. I'll get more details for you if you want.

Cool. That would be great, thanks.

When Ichiro gets home, his mom is waiting at the door. She's really pissed off with him, he can tell.

"Where have you been? Why are you out so late on a school night?"

"Um, I was working, and they wanted me to stay late," Ichiro replies.

"At the diner?"

She is really mad. This is not going to end well.

"Then I went to hang out with some friends," he says. His voice is shaking a bit.

"Don't lie to me, Ichiro. Why are you home so late?" She starts to move closer to him.

"Mom, I have another job." He doesn't want to deal with her anger tonight.

"At that club?" Her face looks like it's going to explode.

"Yes," he says. He moves away quickly because it looks like she's about to hit him.

"I told you no." She's shaking now.

"But I have to," he says and starts walking away.

"No, you do not, and you will not be going back. Do you hear me?"

Everyone on the block can probably hear her.

"I told you, I have to do this right now, Mom. It's part of the plan." He's almost whispering. He sees his mom soften.

"You need to go to sleep. Did you do your class work?"

"Yes, don't worry." He's almost made it to his room now.

She calls out after him. "I sent out some job applications today and went to a temp agency. I think I can get references from a couple of old jobs." She sounds exhausted.

"'Night, Mom. Don't worry," he says again.

Chapter Thirteen

Ichiro arranges to meet up with Lana at a coffee shop on the Drive. Good thing she lives close by. "Hi, darling!" she calls out when she spots him. She looks a lot different out of drag. She has short, curly dark hair and a perfect, triangle-shaped face. Her muscular arms look funny in proportion to her height. Her voice is light, a lot lighter than when she is in drag. "Well, is this how you pictured me?"

"I, uh, I don't know." He's never sure how to answer that kind of question—any answer he gives might be up for a challenge or debate.

"Well, never mind that. Let's get started with you and your performance. What kind of music do you like?"

"A bit of everything."

"Name a campy song that you like."

"'Let's Have a Kiki,'" says Ichiro. He's not sure why he said that.

"What? OMG, that's perfect! But do you have the right attitude? Because you are gonna need it for that song," Lana says. "What is it you like about the song?"

"*Ennui* is one of my favorite words."

"Okaaay...you sound like a weird kid. But that's fine. Now let's look at your face. Oh good, your face is smooth. That's a good start."

"Thanks?"

"Right, so you need to come up with some kind of persona and name. Have you thought about it? Our drag troupe is called the Ono Lab, after Yoko Ono. It's a house of drag artists, so we all have artist names. I'm Yoohoo Kusama, in honor of the artist Yayoi Kusama. You may have noticed that I have polka dots on all my outfits, so that's taken. We also have a drag king named Woo Wu, after the designer Jason Wu. There's also Niki the Saint, after Niki de Saint Phalle, and Taktak Murakami..."

Lana is talking so fast. Ichiro tries hard to stay focused. He knows some of the artists she mentions but not all. He just keeps nodding.

"We need to find something that fits you. Are there some artist personas you like? Take some time to think about it. Do some research. Something spectacular. You know in drag, the bigger the better! Now what about your performance?"

"I've been practicing my dance moves and working on my lip-syncing."

Lana puts a large plastic bag down on the floor. "That's great. We also need to talk outfits. I brought some drag essentials for you. At the Lab, we have extra wigs and outfits from when we first started. You can borrow from these and then slowly build up your own wardrobe. Try them on and choose one wig and one outfit with shoes that you like the best."

Ichiro looks in the bag and sees many pieces of bright-colored fabric. There are also things in there that don't look like clothes at all.

"For makeup, do your face to match your drag persona. Think about the overall design in that way. The colors you choose for your face and your outfit can be colors that the artist likes to use. You can even add artifacts to your outfit that symbolize some of that artist's work. It should be representational of them somehow." Lana hands him a small pouch.

"Here are some makeup basics for you with a couple of paint sticks in there, one for base and the other for highlights."

"This is amazing, Lana. Thank you so much. I really appreciate it."

"I'm going to send you links to some of the best YouTube tutorials for beginners. That's how I got started. Try out some new lewks! For the basics, put on this cap to keep your hair out of the way." She digs into the bag and pulls out something to show Ichiro. "Then use moisturizer to smooth your skin. Glue down your eyebrows with this." She hands him something that looks like a glue stick. "Then apply this foundation paint over your face. Use this highlighting paint stick sparingly. Contouring sponges help blend in the different shades."

"Okay," says Ichiro, typing in a few notes on his phone.

"Drag is all about self-expression. Think of yourself as a blank canvas." Lana does a twirl. And for a brief moment Ichiro pictures her in drag.

"Do powder placements first, then liner. Outline your lips, but make the outlines bigger. Oh, but don't forget the lip balm before starting. Or you'll never get the color off. Then lashes and mascara after your makeup is done."

"Wait, what do I do first? My makeup first and then get dressed?" Ichiro asks.

"Depends on the outfit. If getting into it will wreck your face, put your outfit on first. It'll take you a while at first, but don't rush it. I listen to music while I'm getting ready. Choose a song that fits your persona. It can be that kiki song or something else that might suit you better. Then practice your dance moves and lip-syncing by recording yourself over and over again. If you work hard, you can enter the youth drag contest next month. It's a big tournament for amateur performers who are just getting started."

"But that's too soon," squeaks Ichiro.

"No, you'll be fine, and I'm going to help you. Big prize money. The contest is sponsored by MAC."

"MAC the makeup brand?"

"Yup!"

"Okay, I can do this." He is surprised by the words coming out of his mouth.

"Yes, you can." Lana sounds like she really believes it. Ichiro wishes he had that much confidence in himself.

"My mom will kill me if she finds out."

"We'll keep it our secret, honey. Now, go get yourself a name, pick an outfit, practice a song and come by the Lab in a couple of days. No pressure, ha ha. Everyone is dying to meet you."

"Thanks, Lana."

"Remember, honey, you've got to work hard at

this—but have fun too! Now go on, get a move on," she says, waving him up from his chair.

As Ichiro leaves the coffee shop, he hears Lana call out, "Hate to see you leave, but love to watch you walk away!"

Chapter Fourteen

Ichiro is on his way to meet Lexie and have a look at her cousin's A-liner. It might be perfect for his mom and him to escape in after his graduation. She did just find a new job, but who knows if it will work out? They could move somewhere else and start fresh.

"Hey, Ichiro, this is my cousin Kenzo."

He looks like your average cis West Coast guy. He's got a bit of a scruffy goatee and is wearing jeans with a plaid flannel jacket.

"Lexie tells me you're looking for a camper. Don't know if you've ever heard of an A-liner before, but they're pretty awesome. C'mon in. We keep it parked in the garage most of the time. I pulled it out so I can show you how to set it up. You can have a better look in the daylight."

"Thanks. What year is it?" Ichiro circles around the camper, looking for obvious structural damage.

"It's a 2010 A-Liner Expedition model with two beds on opposite sides, a flush toilet, sink, three-burner range, microwave, refrigerator and air conditioner."

"Does it have a shower?"

"There's an outdoor shower that you can hook up when the weather is nice."

"It looks like it has almost everything we need."

"The table in the dinette area turns into a bed."

He pulls out the table, and it becomes a double bed. "I even mounted a TV in there and hooked up a cheap DVD player. Or you can stream if you have Wi-Fi access."

"It's so awesome." Ichiro is mesmerized. It's in way nicer condition than he expected.

"We only took it out a couple of times before we got too busy with the babies. Thinking of getting something bigger in a few years, when they're older. I'm not in any rush to sell it, so if you're interested let me know, and I'll hold it for you. If you're a friend of Lexie's, then it's golden."

"How much are you looking for?"

He names a number that is lower than Ichiro expected but still out of his reach. His face must give him away.

"Look, kid, I'll give you a bit of a deal if you can at least get me a down payment. It'll help us out too, as we need the cash."

"When do you need to know by?"

"If you could let me know in a couple of weeks, that'd be cool."

"Thanks, Kenzo," Lexie and Ichiro say at the same time. They both laugh.

———·———

Ichiro realizes he has a lot of hustling to do. He phones his auntie Edna and tells her the whole story about his mom and how he's worried about her. His aunt agrees to help him out with a bit of a loan, but he needs to put down three thousand dollars soon for Kenzo to hold it for him. He has some of that saved already from working, but it'll take him a while to earn the rest. He has a couple of weeks to work out the other details of his plan.

It's a long shot, but if he won some money in the drag contest, his troubles would be over. He continues practicing his drag routine at home and soon feels almost ready for his debut. He sends Lana short videos of his makeup experiments and routine. She sends him back some helpful feedback. He still needs a lot of work with lip-syncing. She wants him to do some run-throughs with the Ono Lab in public before the contest. He's meeting the crew this evening. He's really nervous.

"Hey, Ichiro!"

"This is Woo Wu, Niki the Saint and Taktak Murakami," says Lana, now dressed as Yoohoo.

"Everyone, meet...Won Kawara!" Ichiro is wearing a bit from all the outfits that Lana has given him. He hears some snorts from the other performers.

"Honey, you still got some work to do," says Niki the Saint.

"It's her first time. Give her a fucking break," says Woo Wu.

"You look stunning for a baby queen," Taktak says with a wink.

Ichiro is feeling very uncomfortable now.

"Shut up, bitches," says Yoohoo. "Let's get to it. This is how it's going to work. I'll go on and do an intro, and then we'll go in the order I gave you. There won't be that many people here because it's Wednesday, so keep it chill and help out Ichiro, okay?"

"Sure," says Taktak. "Don't worry, babe. It will be all right."

"Ichiro will do one short number before the break. This is just a practice session, everyone, for our upcoming shows," Yoohoo says.

"Don't worry—we usually have just a handful of people on Wednesdays. They like to watch us practice," Woo Wu says.

"Okay." Ichiro feels like he's going to vomit.

"Wait, Ichiro. Do you like boys or girls?" asks Woo Wu.

"Calm down, Woo Wu. It doesn't matter," says Niki the Saint.

"But honey, I want to know if we have a queer boy with us or not. I can't get a vibe," Woo Wu says, pouting.

"Hello! It's because he's nervous." Niki the Saint turns to Ichiro. "Just be your true self," she says.

"I guess it doesn't matter to me," says Ichiro.

"You *guess*? Typical boy behavior," Taktak mumbles.

"Drag is open to everyone," says Yoohoo, extending her arms.

"He's still young—leave him alone," says Niki.

She really is a saint, thinks Ichiro.

"Fight me," says Taktak and does a kung fu move at Woo Wu's face to distract her.

"Ichiro, send me your track so I can cue it up," says Yoohoo.

The others are already onstage and have started. They are killing it, which is making Ichiro even more nervous. He hears his music come on and steps onto the stage, his arms and legs moving everywhere and his mouth moving in a confused lip-sync mess. The bright lights are hot, and his face is blood red. There are only a couple of people in the crowd, and he can tell by the looks on their faces that they are not impressed. He finishes, sweaty and drained.

"You did okay. A little thrown…" says Yoohoo.

"Not bad, but work on your lip-syncing," says Woo Wu. "Like, really. A lot."

Ichiro feels really embarrassed. He can't even remember what happened out there.

"It was your first time, so don't worry." Taktak caresses the back of his hands.

"We all agree you have potential," says Yoohoo.

"More confidence," says Yoohoo. "You gotta own the stage."

Later, when he gets home, Ichiro replies to his auntie Edna's text. She has agreed to lend Ichiro the rest of the money, but not until he's saved up for the down payment. She's trying to teach him how to be fiscally responsible. She wants to know if he's convinced his mom yet.

Think so. I'm going to do it no matter what. So she should just join me. There's a culinary-arts program on the Island that I'm thinking about.

Get your mom to call me.

———·———

He's meeting Lexie at the Elephant Garden Creamery. He's excited to see her but trying to act all chill about it. Confidence is key, as Yoohoo told him.

"Hi," says Lexie. She looks so cute that Ichiro can't help but grin.

"Hey," Ichiro says. He opens the door, and they have a look at the menu on the wall behind the counter.

"Everything sounds so good," she says.

"I'm going for the Mango Coconut Sticky Rice," he says.

"Lemon Yuzu Butter for me." They grab a seat at the wooden table inside.

"Thanks for your help with the trailer. I talked to my aunt, and I think it's going to work out. I'll have the money for it soon."

"That's awesome. My cousin will be happy for you."

Their talk is lighthearted and flirty. Just the kind of first date one would want. Time flies, and before they know it, the shop looks like it's about to close.

"That was fun. Are you busy next weekend?" asks Lexie. "We could hang out."

"Swamped for the next couple of weeks—sorry. I have to visit my aunt on the Island next weekend. And I'm so behind on homework and have more work shifts too." He *hates* saying all this, because it sounds like he doesn't want to see her.

"Oh, okay," she says. She looks sad.

"Can we hang out in a couple of weeks?"

"Yeah, I guess," she says. "I mean, sure."

"I'll walk you home."

"You better." She's smiling again.

As they walk the dark streets, he links arms with her. It's a bit chilly, and they both put their hands in their pockets.

"There's this really good life-drawing class at a place called Basic Inquiry," Ichiro says.

"Oh yeah? That sounds like fun."

"I'll take you there sometime. On Friday evenings they have a long pose session."

"Awesome! I have lots of art materials that I can bring."

They reach the door to her apartment building, an old three-story walk-up just off Main.

"Cool building. I love the stained-glass windows," says Ichiro.

"Me too." She pauses, then says, "Have you ever— oh, forget it." She looks away.

He's glad she stopped. He doesn't know what

she was going to ask. *Have you ever kissed a girl, had sex, been in love?* He doesn't know what he would say. He's feeling so awkward right now. "I'll probably see you at school tomorrow," he says.

"Okay, but just in case." She looks him in the eye, pulls him closer and gives him a light, warm kiss. Ichiro wants a bit more, so he returns another, longer one.

"Good night," she says.

Chapter Fifteen

Tonight is the night. After a couple of months of practice, Ichiro is finally ready to hit the stage. He's making his big debut in the youth drag contest. He's nervous, but he's been practicing with the Ono Lab, and everyone has given him good tips. Be confident, he says to himself. He finally has the right outfit—the hot-pink jumpsuit that he'd gone back to the thrift store to grab, a wide black belt that he found in his mom's closet and a white cowboy hat from the bag Lana gave him. He's going to be doing a jazzed-up version of Miley Cyrus singing "Jolene." He's glad the lyrics aren't too hard to memorize.

After the first two baby drag performers finish, it's his turn. He hears his drag name being announced, but it's all a blur. The lights come up, and he steps out into the middle of the stage. He closes his eyes and then, on the first note of his song, he looks out into the crowd. Everything flashes by so fast. *What? Oh, fuck no.* He thinks he sees Lexie. *Yup.* There she is, with Jia, Chris and even Virat. He freezes. There's some light murmuring in the crowd. He looks offstage at the organizers. They restart the song from the beginning.

Ichiro closes his eyes again. He needs to do this—he *wants* to do this. He starts out slow, but as the music rises he gets into the zone. He's really amped up now. He gets down on his knees and points to everyone in the audience, making a connection with them. The crowd starts to go wild. Someone screams, "I love your pink jumpsuit, baby drag face." He doesn't think about the fact that his friends are out there too.

The Ono Lab is cheering him on, chanting his name. Confidence is on his side now. He's so glad that he asked Yoohoo for advice about boobs. His ample ones are safely protected as he does some acrobatic splits and spins onstage.

Finally Ichiro looks directly at Lexie. She hasn't taken her eyes off him. The song isn't over, but the audio track goes quiet. The room is dark except for the bright spotlight trained on Ichiro. The light follows him as he suddenly jumps out into the audience and slides across the floor. He leaps up onto the bar.

Someone screams, "Yasssss, Queen!" Everyone is snapping their fingers. Ichiro puts up his hands to quiet the screaming. Then he closes his number by singing the final lines of the song a capella.

The members of the Ono Lab look stunned—their mouths are hanging open. Then they are clapping, then hollering. They all get up and give him a standing ovation. That's when it hits Ichiro. His friends! What will they think? He runs to the back of the stage and hides in a dark corner. He's so embarrassed. He peeks out into the crowd. *Yup, they are still all there. Fuck.* He's going to wait backstage until they go. He puts his head in his hands.

"Ichiro! Get out here!" screams Yoohoo.

"No! Leave me alone. I'm sorry."

"Get out here!"

Ichiro knows that Queen Jasmine is going to win first place for sure. There were two other performers who were excellent too. He wants to curl up in a ball and die. The host hops onto the stage with a rather dramatic leap. "And the winner tonight is… Queen Jasmine! Second place goes to Queen… Won Kawara!"

What? Yoohoo pushes him out onto the stage, and he shyly takes a bow.

His head is spinning. He doesn't even hear who won third place. He stumbles into the wings again.

"What's wrong with you?" Taktak exclaims.

"I sucked. How did I end up in second place?" Ichiro says.

"You need a self-esteem reset," says Woo Wu. "You were really good, honey! A rocky start but a brilliant performance!" She kisses Ichiro's cheek.

The best thing about the evening is that with the cash prize, he almost has enough money now for the down payment on the A-liner. The worst thing about the evening is having to explain all this to his friends.

Taktak pokes his head into the far corner of the green room. "Ichiro, what are you doing? Some teenagers are out here, insisting on talking with you."

"Can you tell them this queen wasn't feeling well and went home?"

"Okay, I'll tell them to go away, honey, don't you worry."

Ichiro is exhausted and just wants to fall into bed. What a night. He takes everything off in the changeroom. He shoves it all into a black garbage bag and crams that into his backpack.

He doesn't look at his phone until he's home. There are two texts. One from Chris and one from Jia.

Hey, buddy, do anything fun besides work tonight?

We missed you tonight. We went to a drag show for the first time. You ever been?

No text from Lexie. Ichiro turns off his phone and rolls over in bed.

——.——

The next morning as he gets ready for school, Ichiro decides he'll keep a low profile that day. He hopes he can avoid his friends and even Lexie for a few days. They'll forget about the show eventually. Ichiro decides to walk instead of taking his skateboard. He'll be less noticeable that way. He pulls his hoodie over his head too. At least he doesn't have classes with any of his friends today.

He manages to avoid them for the whole day, but right at three o'clock, as he's packing up to head to work, he sees Chris. And Chris sees him.

Oh crap.

Chris points at Ichiro and starts singing, "*Joleeeeeeeeeeeene…*"

Ichiro rushes away, but Chris catches up.

"Where are you heading to in such a hurry, buddy?" Chris taps him on the shoulder. He has a huge grin on his face.

"Work, gotta go." Ichiro runs to catch the bus. He looks out the bus window and sees Chris looking a bit confused. He feels bad. He just doesn't want to talk about it. It would take too much energy to explain everything to them right now.

When he gets home from the café, his mother is waiting for him. "We need to talk," she says and motions toward the kitchen table. He sits down. Her tone sounds serious.

"Look, I talked to Auntie Edna, and she told me about your plan."

"Mom, it's perfect. I'll have the money for a down payment. Auntie Edna is going to lend me the rest and let us pay it back when we can. There's a pop-up camper—"

"Stop, Ichiro. Listen, I'm fine now. I like my new job, and I'm getting more hours. The pay's good. And I need to live in the city—you know that."

"But I've already—"

"Ichiro, you don't make plans for the both of us, okay?!"

"But…" Ichiro inhales deeply. What is he going to do now?

"I talked to Auntie Edna and agreed that she can still lend you the money, but you have to promise to pay her back on time. You're a young man now, and you have your own dreams. If you want to live on the Island in a trailer, I'm not going to stop you."

"Really?" He can't believe his mom is being so understanding. He also realizes that she has just called him a young man.

"Yes. This, you—it's all new for me. I don't know... what. I need some time."

"You're not going to come with me, but Mom—"

"I can look after myself. Don't worry about me. And I have to be ready to leave if Grandma calls. I need to be close to the international airport."

"Well, don't worry about me then. I'll be fine."

"You are very headstrong and you never listen to me anyway." She laughs.

Ichiro laughs too. "Sorry, Mom."

"You do okay on your own. I'm sorry I couldn't look after you or be there for you much."

"It's okay, I know you were busy."

"Work out everything with Auntie, okay?"

"Thanks, Mom." Ichiro gives his mom a big hug.

He can't believe he's going to pursue his dream of taking culinary classes and living on his own. The only thing that sucks is he'll miss Chris and Jia, and then there's Lexie too. As soon as he finally meets someone he really likes, he's going to leave. *Shit.*

When he gets to school the next day, Lexie pulls him aside. Chris and Jia come and join them.

"What's going on with you?" Lexie asks.

"We all know it was you up there," says Chris. "You were awesome, man."

"You should have told us," says Jia. "But yeah, I second Chris. You were epic!"

"Yeah, why didn't you say anything?" asks Lexie. She looks sad.

"I'm sorry. I've just been so busy. I almost have enough money for your cousin's trailer. I needed extra shifts and wasn't getting home until really late. I should have told you all what I was up to."

"Okay, I guess we forgive you. That was a really great show. Tell us everything!" Lexie says, linking arms with him. As they all make their way to class, Ichiro tells them about Yoohoo and the Ono Lab. At lunch in the cafeteria, he fills them in on the rest.

"There's something else I need to let you all know," says Ichiro. He locks eyes with Lexie. "I'm thinking about going to university on the Island."

"Oh, really? Why haven't we heard about this before?" asks Jia. "What else are you keeping from us?"

"Nothing, that's it. They have a culinary-arts certificate program at Greater Victoria University. I'm probably going to move the trailer over there. Saves me from having to rent a place," says Ichiro.

Lexie smiles. "I didn't mention this either, but I have a friend who lives over there. We're both planning to apply to the visual arts program at GVU too."

"Aw! It's like you two were meant to be together," says Jia. She's teasing, but Ichiro thinks she might be right. He looks at Lexie. She's still smiling.

"So jelly," Chris says with a sigh.

"We should all go. What are your plans after graduation?" Ichiro asks. He suddenly realizes how much he will miss his friends.

"Never thought of anything much. Probably get a job like my parents did," says Chris.

"Yeah, me too. How can I afford uni?" Jia moans.

"Get a student loan, work part-time, and come to GVU with us. Do some research and see what they offer. You can take something cool," says Ichiro.

"Can I even do that?" asks Chris.

"Yeah, how?" says Jia.

"We'll help you figure it out," says Ichiro. "Then

when school's out, we can take the camper and travel. Wherever we want to go!"

"Let destiny fill our worlds with opportunities!" says Lexie.

They all fist-bump. "To destiny!"

Acknowledgments

Huge thanks and love to my family for putting up with me forever and always. Big love to my TWS writing friends—Lindsay, Kait, Nikki, Christine, Jennifer and Erica—for our writerly discussions over the years. To my beloved lifelong friends from college—Ann Marie, Ish, Gemma, Audrey, Christine and Louise. I know you have my back. Thank you to Oliv Howe (EmpressX) and all of the amazing drag performers that I've worked with. You are all brilliant. Shout-out to the community for supporting your local drag artists and LGBTQ+ spaces. We appreciate you.

A ton of thanks to Tash McAdam for the nudge of encouragement and Tanya Trafford (editor extraordinaire) for all of your wonderful help and advice. More thanks to: Doeun Rivendell for your terrific support in bringing it to the finish line in a spectacular way, Olivia Gutjahr for the fantastic help with marketing, Ella Collier for the wonderful cover and interior design work, and of course tremendous gratitude to Orca Book Publishers for publishing my first baby.

C.A. Tanaka is a trans masculine multiracial writer of Japanese, Chinese, Indonesian and Scottish descent. A graduate of The Writer's Studio program at Simon Fraser University, they have a BFA in intermedia from Emily Carr University of Art + Design and, in 2017, were awarded a fully funded literary residency at the Banff Centre for Arts and Creativity. C.A. is the executive director for the Storytelling with Drag Queens Foundation, a local non-profit organization with a mandate to promote diversity and inclusion in literacy for children, teens and adults. They live in Vancouver, British Columbia, on the unceded ancestral homelands of the xʷməθkʷəy̓əm (Musqueam), Sḵwx̱wú7mesh (Squamish), and səlílwətaɬ (Tsleil-Waututh) Nations.